This book belongs to

_____

For Papa. Thank you.

Happy Harper: Grandpa Comes Home

Text and Illustrations copyright ©2022 by M. Michelle Derosier

Library of Congress Control Number: Pending

Paperback ISBN: 978-1-954427-04-4
Hardcover ISBN: 978-1-954427-03-7
e-Book ISBN: 978-1-954427-05-1

First Edition, 2022

Published by In DisQovery Press, Wilmington, DE

https://www.happyharperbooks.com

Happy Harper

Grandpa Comes Home

Kayla Marie Pierre

Illustrated by Fathima Hakkim

Harper wished she could shrink the world.

She wanted to make it smaller
so her grandpa would live closer.

Harper could walk the three blocks
to Mrs. Raul's bodega.

She could hop in a car to visit her
favorite cousins for Christmas.

But her one and only grandpa was too **far** away for a walk or car ride.

Sometimes when
Harper swam in the
neighborhood pool,

she pretended to cross
the **mighty** ocean,
all the way to Grandpa in Haiti.

She imagined gliding past
fish friends on their way to school—

and catching a ride
on the back of
their teacher, Mr. Whale.

Kicking harder and faster with each stroke, she hurried closer to Grandpa.

But when she stepped out of the pool, Grandpa remained far away.

Sharing phone calls and photos with Grandpa was fun.
But Harper wanted to see his dark brown eyes twinkle
— and to giggle when he made
his bushy eyebrows dance.

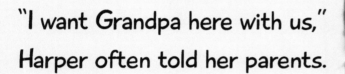

"I want Grandpa here with us,"
Harper often told her parents.

"Is Grandpa coming today?"
she asked almost every day.

The answer was "No, not yet"
when Harper picked dogwoods
with her parents in the spring.

It was "No, but *SOON*"
with the first bite of blueberry
ice cream in the SUMMER.

It was "No, but don't worry" when
the three of them splashed through
puddles in the fall.

And it was "No, but any day now" when
they tossed snowballs in the winter.

With each passing season,
Harper dreamed of the day
she would hug her grandpa.

Finally, the day had arrived.
"Grandpa is coming to live with us!"
Harper shouted for all to hear.

Harper and her parents prepared
for Grandpa's arrival as busily
as   tending to their hive.

Harper's mother sifted flour and creamed butter
for pineapple upside-down cake—Grandpa's favorite.

Her father decorated the living room with
streamers and a large banner: Byenveni!

And Harper was working hard
on a gift to welcome Grandpa.

"Mommy, I need—" Harper's mother
handed her a big sheet of paper.

"Daddy, what about—" Harper's father laid
out a bright bouquet of crayons.

Harper drew slowly.

She colored in the sunny blue sky.
The rich brown soil of Grandpa's vegetable garden.
The cherry-red door of his family's farmhouse.
And the lush green forest that covered
the mountains in the distance.

"Finished! Time to go!" Harper announced at last.

They hopped on and off three trains to reach JFK airport.

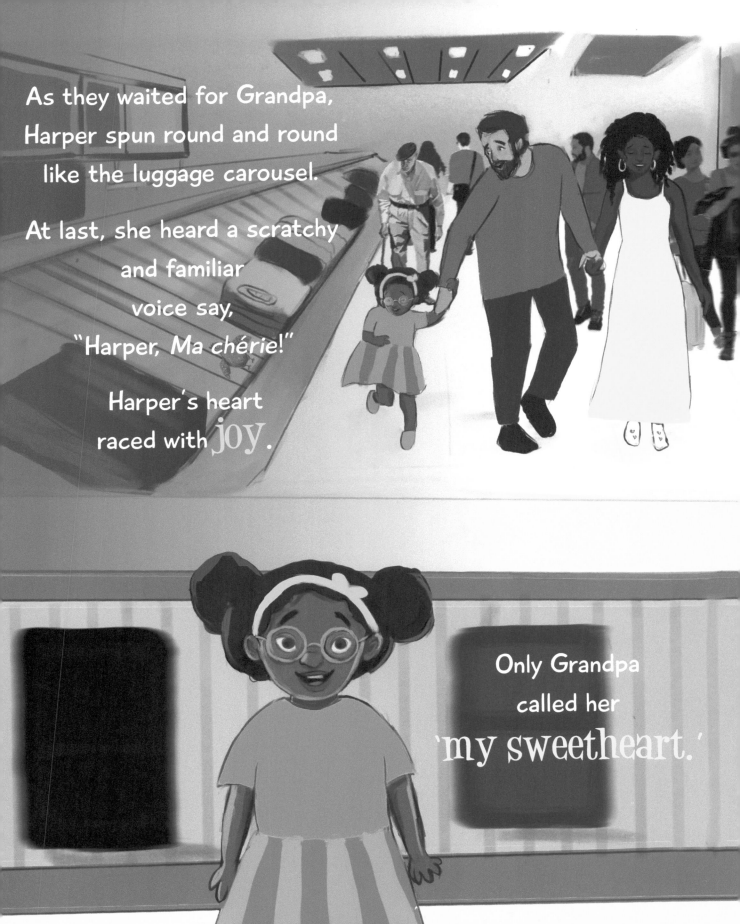

As they waited for Grandpa,
Harper spun round and round
like the luggage carousel.

At last, she heard a scratchy
and familiar
voice say,
"Harper, *Ma chérie!*"

Harper's heart
raced with joy.

Only Grandpa
called her
'my sweetheart.'

Harper flew into his arms.

"Grandpa!" she roared, forgetting
to use her inside voice.

Harper hugged him tightly.
His soft whiskers tickled her cheek.

Harper's father shook
Grandpa's hand
and slowly said
the word they had
practiced all week,
"*Byenveni!*
Welcome!"

Harper's mother
laughed and cried
when she hugged
her father and
kissed his cheek.

Harper held on to her grandpa
for the long cab ride home.

Back in the family's apartment, she curled up
on the sofa and snuggled next to him.

They traded stories of happy
moments they had missed sharing.

Grandpa's eyes glistened when he gently unwrapped her gift.

"*Tankou lakay*. Just like home," Grandpa said.

Harper frowned. "But, Grandpa, you *are* home," she said. "Your new home with us ... *forever.*"

"Yes, home with my *family*," Grandpa said.

Harper climbed onto his lap and wrapped
him in a hug bigger than a whale.

"I love you, Grandpa," she said.
"Near and far."

Author's Note

Psst! Hi there, Reader!

Thanks for spending time with Happy Harper. What did you like most about the story?

While you were reading, did you notice some clues about Happy Harper's favorite animal?

There's one hidden in every scene.

Here's where they are.

Pages:

1. On the chair
2. Crossing the street
3. In the gift box
4. Between the gift boxes
5. In the pool
6. PLOT TWIST! There's TWO: in the ocean & in the sky
7. In the ocean
8. In a pool float tube
9. Eavesdropping on Harper's phone call (rude!)
10. In the grass by the streetlamp
11. By the hydrant (in case there's a fire)
12. In the bushes
13. Snownimal (Snow + Animal)
14. Snuggled up with Harper
15. PT! Hanging by the window (not helping clean!) & one of the toys

16. TRICKY! There are THREE: on the fridge, in the picture on the fridge, & the couch
17. Sitting in his favorite chair (thinking about life)
18. On a white piece of paper
19. Riding the train
20. Taking a joy ride on the luggage carousel
21 & 22. In the wheelchair wheel (that's dangerous!)
23. Standing on Grandpa's feet
24. Sitting down (forgot your seatbelt!)
25. Back to favorite chair
26. Grandpa, the gift is from both of us!
27 & 28. Peeking out the red door
29 & 30. TRICKY! There are THREE: in the red door, on the welcome mat, & in the framed photo

I bet you found all of them. I don't think the adults did. Maybe you can read *Grandpa Comes Home* again and help them!

Want some puzzles and coloring pages? Ask your family's permission to check out *www.happyharperbooks.com*.

So good chatting with you! Look for the next *Happy Harper* book coming soon.

— KMP —

This love story is a heartfelt thank you to my grandpa, Calixte, and to all the fathers, grandfathers, and father figures who sacrifice every day for their families. This is especially for those who are overlooked, disrespected, and disregarded by a world that measures a person's value by their net worth.

The world can never see their true value, but we do. It's in the way they provide stability, care, and comfort— even from a distance.

Happy Harper Grandpa Comes Home is dedicated to them: The immigrants, the "boat people," the janitors, the cab drivers, the cafeteria workers, the school bus drivers, the day laborers...to all of the ones who work hard, day in and day out, to invest in a better future for their children and grandchildren.

We see you.
We appreciate you.
We love you.

CPSIA information can be obtained
at www.ICGtesting.com
Printed in the USA
LVHW071742140222
711102LV00012B/742